Dedication

This book is dedicated to all the girls that want to rule the world!

Written by P.E. Barnes and Illustrated by Aria Jones

Sierra is the owner of a popular world class salon spa in downtown Chicago with other locations. Her salon provides hair care, manicures, pedicures, massages and relaxation for her clients.

Sierra's passion for beauty started at a young age, she loved styling her baby dolls hair.

As a teenager Sierra was hired to work at a beauty salon as an assistant. She was mentored by the best stylists in the salon and she was inspired to go to cosmetology school.

Sierra attended cosmetology school, a school that trains students to become licensed in hair, nails, makeup and some skin care. She graduated from cosmetology school and she took her state exam to become a licensed hair stylist.

Sierra rented a booth at a salon, and the salon gave her an opportunity to build her clientele.

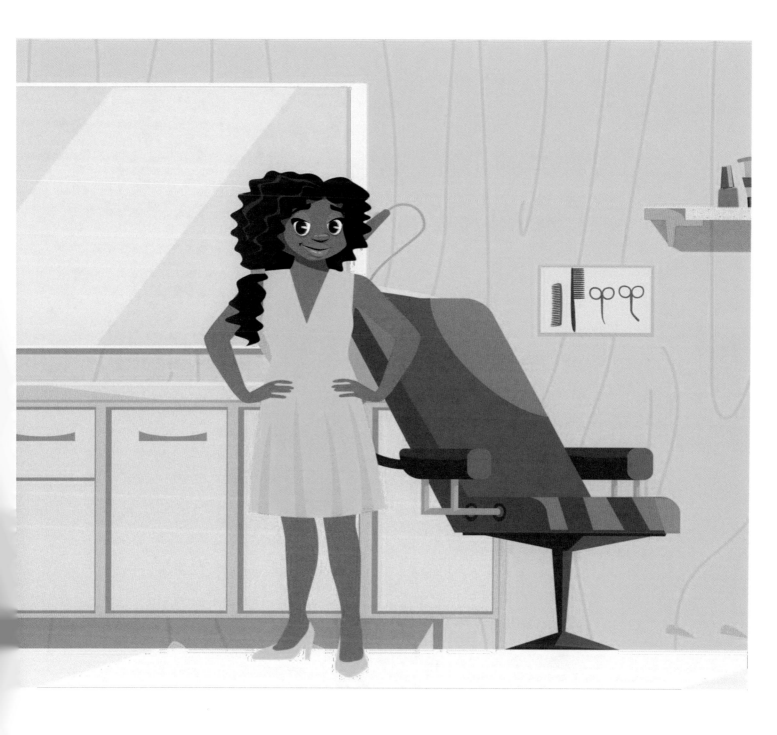

After years of working at the salon, Sierra has built a large clientele. She was outgrowing the chair she was renting at the salon.

Sierra saved a down payment to buy her own salon. She found a mixed-use building that would allow her to live in an apartment and have her business in the same building.

Sierra made her salon a full service salon and spa. The salon offered hair, facials, massages, and nail services. The grand opening was very successful.

Sierra was able to hire other people such as other hairstylist, nail technician, massage therapist and an esthetician.

Sierra's salon was very successful and she opened several other locations. She was able to create wealth for herself and others.

The
End

Vocabulary

Clientele- customers of a shop, bar, or establishment.

Hire- to employ someone or pay someone to do a particular job.

Mentor-a more experienced or knowledgeable person advises and helps a less experienced person.

Downpayment-a lump sum payment one makes on an asset financed with debt.

Mixed-used building- a building with an apartment and work space.

Esthetician- skin care therapists, they provide facials, waxing, body treatments etc.

About the Author

P.E. Barnes is a real estate investor in Chicago. She is passionate about educating children about financial literacy. She is a wife and mother of two young boys that inspired this book series.

For bookings or inquiries email: littleowners@gmail.com

Made in the USA
Monee, IL
24 October 2020